Snow Rabbit, Spring Rabbit

A Book of Changing Seasons

Il Sung Na

ALFRED A. KNOPF
NEW YORK

When snow falls to the ground
and all the trees are bare,
everyone knows it's winter . . .

. . . including the rabbit.

Some fly away from the cold.

Some have a long,
cozy sleep where they live.

Some swim to warmer waters,

While some have
a thick woolly coat . . . .

. . . they can stay
in the snow!

Some gather
extra food for winter,

While some travel far . . . .

. . . . to find things to eat.

Some stay very still,

While some keep busy,

moving fast and staying warm!

But when the snow has melted
and the trees are in bloom . . .

. . . everyone knows it's spring!

Including the rabbit.

For my family

THIS IS A BORZOI BOOK PUBLISHED BY ALFRED A. KNOPF

Copyright © 2010 by Il Sung Na

All rights reserved. Published in the United States by Alfred A. Knopf,
an imprint of Random House Children's Books, a division of Random House, Inc., New York.

Knopf, Borzoi Books, and the colophon are registered trademarks of Random House, Inc. Originally published
in slightly different form in Great Britain as *Brrrr: A Book of Winter* by Meadowside Children's Books, London, in 2010.

Visit us on the Web! www.randomhouse.com/kids

Educators and librarians, for a variety of teaching tools, visit us at
www.randomhouse.com/teachers

Library of Congress Cataloging-in-Publication Data is available upon request.
ISBN 978-0-375-86786-6 (trade) — ISBN 978-0-375-96786-3 (lib. bdg.)

The illustrations in this book were created by combining handmade painterly textures with
digitally generated layers, which were then compiled in Adobe Photoshop.

MANUFACTURED IN CHINA
January 2011
10 9 8 7 6 5 4 3 2 1
First American Edition